# AXEL SCHEFFLER

## MACMILLAN CHILDREN'S BOOKS

First published 2006 in *Mother Goose's Nursery Rhymes* by Macmillan Children's Books

...llection published 2007 by Macmillan Children's Books

...f Macmillan Publishers Limited

...London N1 9RR

Associated... ...the world

...w.pa...macmillan.com

ISBN... ...78-0-230-...

Text copyright © Macmillan Children's Books 2006, 2007

Illustrations copyright © Axel Scheffler 2006, 2007.

The right of Axel Scheffler to be identified as the

3 5 7 9 8 6 4

A CIP catalogue record for this book is available from the British Library.

Printed in Belgium

# CONTENTS

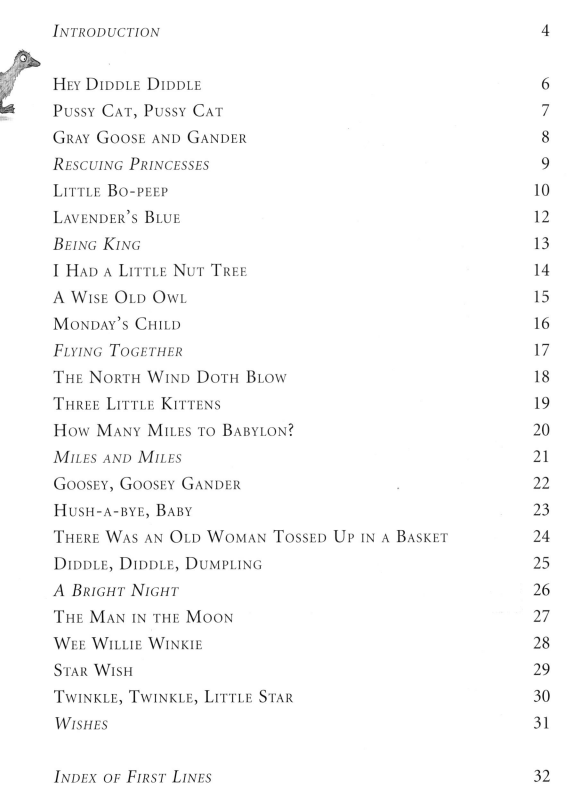

One springtime Mother Goose laid three eggs. The first one to hatch was a boy. He had big flat feet and he was noisy. His mummy called him Boo.

One week later the second egg hatched. She was a girl. She had very flappy wings, and was almost as noisy as Boo. Her mummy called her Lucy.

They had to wait one more week for the last egg to hatch. It was another boy. He was shy and dreamy. His mummy called him Small. Boo, Lucy and Small. Mother Goose was very proud of them.

Mother Goose taught her goslings how to do all the things that geese do: how to nibble at the soft wet grass; how to swim up and down the great wide river; how to duck their heads under the water looking for waterweed; how to sleep on one leg on the riverbank. That was hard.

It wasn't easy looking after goslings.

So Mother Goose started to tell them rhymes: rhymes for playtime, rhymes with actions and rhymes to lull them to sleep.

After that, whenever the goslings argued about what to play, or splashed in puddles instead of doing their flying practice, or didn't want to go to bed, Mother Goose told them a rhyme. She knew all sorts of rhymes that were just right for telling to sleepy goslings. They were such good rhymes that other mother geese started telling them to their goslings, too – and now all their favourite bedtime rhymes are gathered together in this book for families everywhere to enjoy.

# Hey Diddle Diddle

Hey diddle diddle,

The cat and the fiddle,

The cow jumped over the moon;

The little dog laughed

To see such sport,

And the dish ran away with the spoon.

# Pussy Cat, Pussy Cat

Pussy cat, pussy cat, where have you been?

I've been to London to look at the queen.

Pussy cat, pussy cat, what did you there?

I frightened a little mouse under her chair.

# Gray Goose and Gander

Gray goose and gander
    Waft your wings together,
And carry the good king's daughter
    Over the one-strand river.

"That's what I'm going to do when I grow up," said Boo. "I'm going to carry princesses over rivers."

"I thought you were going to be king," said Mother Goose.

"That's later on," said Boo.

"I'll help you carry them," said Lucy. "You can't carry a whole princess on your own."

"But I'd fly faster than you," said Boo, "so the princess would fall down and go splosh into the river."

"Then I'd have to rescue her," said Small.

"We'd all have to rescue her," said Boo. "Then we'd take her to the king."

"And he'd be really grateful, wouldn't he, Mummy?" said Lucy. "And he'd pay us lots of money."

"He'd probably be more grateful if you hadn't dropped her in the river," said Mother Goose.

"We'd flap our wings at her to dry her out," said Boo.

"Well that's all right, then," said Mother Goose.

# Little Bo-peep

Little Bo-peep has lost her sheep,
And can't tell where to find them;
Leave them alone, and they'll come home,
And bring their tails behind them.

Little Bo-peep fell fast asleep,
And dreamt she heard them bleating;
But when she awoke, she found it a joke,
For they were still all fleeting.

Then up she took her little crook,
Determined for to find them;
She found them indeed, but it made her heart bleed,
For they'd left their tails behind them.

It happened one day, as Bo-peep did stray
Into a meadow hard by,
There she espied their tails side by side,
All hung on a tree to dry.

She heaved a sigh, and wiped her eye,
And over the hillocks went rambling,
And tried what she could, as a shepherdess should,
To tack again each to its lambkin.

# Lavender's Blue

Lavender's blue, diddle, diddle,
    Lavender's green;
When I am king, diddle, diddle,
    You shall be queen.

Call up your men, diddle, diddle,
    Set them to work,
Some to the plough, diddle, diddle,
    Some to the cart.

Some to make hay, diddle, diddle,
    Some to thresh corn,
Whilst you and I, diddle, diddle,
    Keep ourselves warm.

"When I'm king," said Boo, "I'll set you all to work. I'll sit on the riverbank, and you'll have to fetch weed for me to eat, and bring it on a silver platter."

"You'll get very fat," said Mother Goose, "if you don't run around and swim."

"And you won't be able to jump in puddles," said Lucy.

"Kings aren't allowed to jump in puddles," said Small.

"Are kings allowed to play games?" asked Boo.

"Only chess," said Lucy. "And crosswords."

"And they have to be in a bad mood all day long, and make up rules for everyone," said Small.

"When are you going to be king?" asked Lucy.

"Oh, not for ages," said Boo. "I'll let you know."

# I Had a Little Nut Tree

I had a little nut tree,
    Nothing would it bear
But a silver nutmeg
    And a golden pear;
The King of Spain's daughter
    Came to visit me,
And all for the sake
    Of my little nut tree.

## A Wise Old Owl

A wise old owl sat in an oak,

The more he heard the less he spoke;

The less he spoke the more he heard.

Why aren't we all like that wise old bird?

# Monday's Child

Monday's child is fair of face,

Tuesday's child is full of grace,

Wednesday's child is full of woe,

Thursday's child has far to go,

Friday's child is loving and giving,

Saturday's child works hard for his living,

And the child that is born on the Sabbath day

Is bonny and blithe, and good and gay.

"What day was I born on, Mummy?" asked Small.

"You hatched out on a Thursday," said Mother Goose.

"Thursday's child has far to go," said Small. "Where have I got to go?"

"Somewhere hot and sunny for the winter, I should think," said Mother Goose. "Geese fly hundreds of miles in the winter."

"What day was I born on, Mummy?" asked Lucy.

"Thursday, the same as Small," said Mother Goose. "You all hatched out on Thursdays, one week after another."

"So we've all got far to go, then?" said Small.

"Yes," said Mother Goose.

"Can we all go together?" asked Small.

"Of course!" said Mother Goose. "Geese always fly together."

"That's all right, then," said Small.

# The North Wind Doth Blow

The north wind doth blow,
And we shall have snow,
And what will poor robin do then?
    Poor thing.
He'll sit in a barn,
And keep himself warm,
And hide his head under his wing.
    Poor thing.

# Three Little Kittens

Three little kittens they lost their mittens,
    And they began to cry,
Oh, mother dear, we sadly fear
    That we have lost our mittens.
What! lost your mittens, you naughty kittens!
    Then you shall have no pie.
    Mee-ow, mee-ow, mee-ow.
    No, you shall have no pie.

The three little kittens they found their mittens,
    And they began to cry,
Oh, mother dear, see here, see here,
    For we have found our mittens.
Put on your mittens, you silly kittens,
    And you shall have some pie.
    Purr-r, purr-r, purr-r,
    Oh, let us have some pie.

# How Many Miles to Babylon?

How many miles to Babylon?

Three score miles and ten.

Can I get there by candlelight?

Yes, and back again.

If your heels are nimble and light,

You may get there by candlelight.

"How far is a mile?" asked Boo.

"A mile is a long way to waddle," said Mother Goose.

"Is it as far as that gate-post?" asked Small.

"It's much further than that," said Mother Goose.

"Gosh," said Small.

"So, how far is three score miles and ten?" asked Lucy.

"That's even further," said Mother Goose.

"Could we get there by candlelight?" asked Boo.

"Geese don't have candles," said Mother Goose. "But we could get there by flying. Geese can fly ever so far."

"Flying's too hard," said Small. "I'm never going to fly."

"You just have to practise," said Mother Goose. "Then you can fly anywhere you want."

"Even to Babylon?" asked Lucy.

"Even to Babylon," said Mother Goose.

So they all practised flapping their wings.

# Goosey, Goosey Gander

Goosey, goosey gander,

    Whither shall I wander?

Upstairs and downstairs

    And in my lady's chamber.

There I met an old man

    Who would not say his prayers.

I took him by the left leg

    And threw him down the stairs.

# Hush-a-bye, Baby

Hush-a-bye, baby, on the tree top,

When the wind blows the cradle will rock;

When the bough breaks the cradle will fall,

Down will come baby, cradle and all.

# There Was an Old Woman Tossed Up in a Basket

There was an old woman tossed up in a basket,

Seventeen times as high as the moon;

Where she was going I couldn't but ask it,

For in her hand she carried a broom.

Old woman, old woman, old woman, quoth I,

Where are you going to up so high?

To brush the cobwebs off the sky!

May I go with you?

Aye, by-and-by.

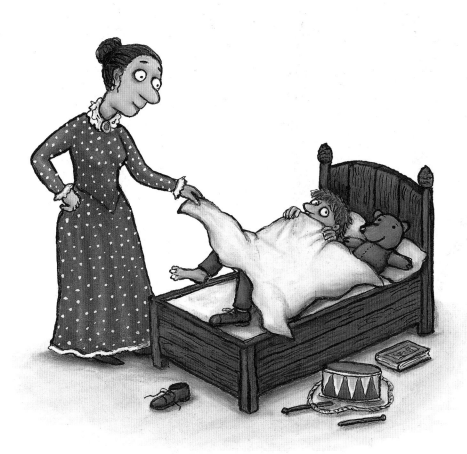

# Diddle, Diddle, Dumpling

Diddle, diddle, dumpling, my son John,
Went to bed with his trousers on;
One shoe off, and one shoe on,
Diddle, diddle, dumpling, my son John.

I t was a bright night, with the moon shining fat and round in the sky.

"Have you noticed how the moon gets bigger and smaller?" asked Mother Goose. The goslings had. "Sometimes it's big and fat like this, then it gets smaller and smaller, till all you can see is a thin little crescent moon."

"Then it gets big again," said Small.

"That's right," said Mother Goose.

"Mummy," said Lucy, "where does the Man in the Moon go when the moon gets too small for him?"

"He comes down to Earth," said Mother Goose, "and goes on holiday to Norwich."

"Why does he go to Norwich?" asked Boo.

"He likes it there," said Mother Goose. "Except for one time, when he came down too soon. There's a rhyme about it . . ."

# The Man in the Moon

The man in the moon
Came down too soon,
And asked his way to Norwich;
He went by the south,
And burnt his mouth
With supping cold plum porridge.

# Wee Willie Winkie

Wee Willie Winkie runs through the town,
Upstairs and downstairs in his night-gown,
Rapping at the window, crying through the lock,
Are the children all in bed, for now it's eight o'clock?

# Twinkle, Twinkle, Little Star

Twinkle, twinkle, little star,
How I wonder what you are!
Up above the world so high,
Like a diamond in the sky.

## Star Wish

Star light, star bright,

First star I see tonight,

I wish I may, I wish I might,

Have the wish I wish tonight.

I t was bedtime. The goslings were looking up at the stars.

"What do you wish, Lucy?" asked Boo.

"I wish I was a ballerina," said Lucy.

"Geese can't be ballerinas," said Boo, "can they, Mummy?"

"They can if they wish hard enough," said Mother Goose.

"What do you wish, Small?" asked Lucy.

"I wish I could fly," said Small.

"But you can fly, silly," said Lucy. "You're a goose!"

"Oh, yes," said Small. "I forgot."

"What do you wish, Mummy?" asked Boo.

"I wish we could all get some sleep," said Mother Goose.

So they did.

# Index of First Lines